THE LEGEND OF
 THE BLUEBONNET

THE LEGEND OF THE BLUEBONNET

AN OLD TALE OF TEXAS

RETOLD AND ILLUSTRATED BY

TOMIE dePAOLA

HOUGHTON MIFFLIN COMPANY

BOSTON

ATLANTA   DALLAS   GENEVA, ILLINOIS   PALO ALTO   PRINCETON

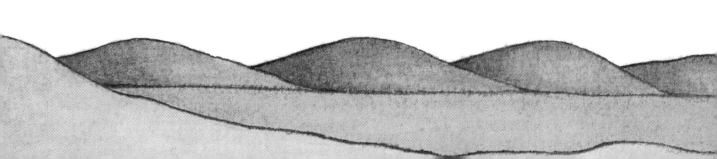

For MARGARET LOOPER,
who introduced me to the tale.

T.deP.

Acknowledgments

Grateful acknowledgment is made for permission to excerpt and/or reprint original or copyrighted materials, as follows:

The Legend of the Bluebonnet, text and illustrations copyright © 1983 by Tomie dePaola. Reprinted by arrangement with The Putnam & Grosset Group. All rights reserved.

Photography

36-37 The Bettmann Archive **37** National Museum of American Art/Art Resource, NY **38-39** Kunio Owaki/The Stock Market

Houghton Mifflin Edition, 1997
Copyright © 1997 by Houghton Mifflin Company. All rights reserved.

Printed in the U.S.A.

ISBN-13: **978-0-395-81175-7**   ISBN-10: **0-395-81775-9**

89-B-08 07

"Great Spirits,
the land is dying. Your People are dying, too,"
the long line of dancers sang.
"Tell us what we have done to anger you.
End this drought. Save your People.
Tell us what we must do so you will send the rain
that will bring back life."

For three days,
the dancers danced to the sound of the drums,
and for three days, the People called Comanche
watched and waited.
And even though the hard winter was over,
no healing rains came.

9

Drought and famine are hardest
on the very young and the very old.

Among the few children left
was a small girl named She-Who-Is-Alone.
She sat by herself watching the dancers.
In her lap was a doll made from buckskin—a warrior doll.
The eyes, nose and mouth were painted on
with the juice of berries. It wore beaded leggings
and a belt of polished bone.
On its head were brilliant blue feathers
from the bird who cries "Jay-jay-jay."
She loved her doll very much.

"Soon," She-Who-Is-Alone said to her doll,
"the shaman will go off alone to the top of the hill
 to listen for the words of the Great Spirits.
 Then, we will know what to do so that once more
 the rains will come and the Earth will be green and alive.
 The buffalo will be plentiful
 and the People will be rich again."

As she talked, she thought of the mother who made
the doll, of the father who brought the blue feathers.
She thought of the grandfather and the grandmother
she had never known. They were all like shadows.
It seemed long ago that they had died from the famine.
The People had named her and cared for her.
The warrior doll was the only thing she had left
from those distant days.

"The sun is setting," the runner called
as he ran through camp. "The shaman is returning."
The People gathered in a circle and the shaman spoke.

"I have heard the words of the Great Spirits," he said.
"The People have become selfish.
For years, they have taken from the Earth
without giving anything back.
The Great Spirits say the People must sacrifice.
We must make a burnt offering
of the most valued possession among us.
The ashes of this offering shall then be scattered to
the four points of the Earth, the Home of the Winds.
When this sacrifice is made,
drought and famine will cease.
Life will be restored to the Earth and to the People!"

The People sang a song of thanks to the Great Spirits
for telling them what they must do.

"I'm sure it is not my new bow
  that the Great Spirits want," a warrior said.
"Or my special blanket," a woman added,
  as everyone went to their tipis to talk and think over
  what the Great Spirits had asked.

Everyone, that is, except She-Who-Is-Alone.
She held her doll tightly to her heart.
"You," she said, looking at the doll.
"You are my most valued possession.
It is you the Great Spirits want."
And she knew what she must do.

18

As the council fires died out
and the tipi flaps began to close,
the small girl returned to the tipi,
where she slept, to wait.

The night outside was still except for the distant sound
of the night bird with the red wings.
Soon everyone in the tipi was asleep, except She-Who-Is-Alone.
Under the ashes of the tipi fire one stick still glowed.
She took it and quietly crept out into the night.

She ran to the place on the hill
where the Great Spirits had spoken to the shaman.
Stars filled the sky, but there was no moon.
"O Great Spirits," She-Who-Is-Alone said,
"here is my warrior doll. It is the only thing I have
from my family who died in this famine.
It is my most valued possession. Please accept it."

Then, gathering twigs,
she started a fire with the glowing firestick.
The small girl watched
 as the twigs began to catch and burn.

She thought of her grandmother and grandfather,
her mother and father and all the People—
their suffering, their hunger.
And before she could change her mind,
she thrust the doll into the fire.

She watched until the flames died down
and the ashes had grown cold.
Then, scooping up a handful, She-Who-Is-Alone
scattered the ashes to the Home of the Winds,
the North and the East, the South and the West.

And there she fell asleep
until the first light of the morning sun woke her.

She looked out over the hill
and stretching out from all sides, where the ashes had fallen,
the ground was covered with flowers—beautiful flowers,
as blue as the feathers in the hair of the doll,
as blue as the feathers of the bird who cries "Jay-jay-jay."

When the People came out of their tipis,
they could scarcely believe their eyes.
They gathered on the hill with She-Who-Is-Alone
to look at the miraculous sight.
There was no doubt about it,
the flowers were a sign of forgiveness
from the Great Spirits.

And as the People sang
and danced their thanks to the Great Spirits,
a warm rain began to fall
and the land began to live again.
From that day on,
the little girl was known by another name—
"One-Who-Dearly-Loved-Her-People."

And every spring,
the Great Spirits remember the sacrifice of a little girl
and fill the hills and valleys of the land, now called Texas,
with the beautiful blue flowers.

Even to this very day.

Author's Note

The bluebonnet is a form of wild lupine. It is known by other names, too, such as Lupine, Buffalo Clover, Wolf Flower, and "El Conejo"—the rabbit. But its most familiar name, Bluebonnet, probably began when the white settlers moved to Texas. The lovely blue flowers they saw growing wild were thought to resemble the bonnets worn by many of the women to shield them from the hot Texas sun.

The suggestion to do a book for children on the origin of the Texas state flower came to me from Margaret Looper, a reading consultant in Huntsville, Texas. Gathering folktale material is always interesting, but more so when the suggestion to "look at" a tale comes from a friend. Margaret sent me a copy and I cannot thank her enough, for I was immediately drawn to it.

Then, with tireless effort, Margaret kept me supplied with as many versions as she could locate; and during one long New Hampshire winter, my mailbox was filled with information and pictures of that lovely spring wildflower.

Margaret also helped me find out about the Comanche People, especially details about their early life in Texas before it became impossible for these brave people to share the land with the settlers and they were expelled or had to flee.

When doing a book based on legend involving real people, it becomes a drive to find out as much as possible about their customs and way of life in an effort to portray as accurate and full a picture as possible. In this search, one comes upon information that fascinates. One point especially interesting to me was that the Comanche People did not have a concept of one god or Great Spirit. They worshiped many spirits equally, and each one represented a special skill or trait. They prayed to the Deer Spirit for agility, the Wolf Spirit for ferocity, the Eagle Spirit for strength, and to the important Buffalo Spirit to send them buffalo for the hunt. The Crow Spirit was evil. Therefore, in my retelling, the People pray to the Great Spirits collectively.

Even though the legend of the bluebonnet is a tale about the origin of a flower, for me it is more a tale of the courage and sacrifice of a young person. She-Who-Is-Alone's act of thrusting her beloved doll into the fire to save her people represents the decisive sort of action that many young people are capable of, the kind of selfless action that creates miracles.

T.deP.

PAPERBACK **PLUS**
· SERIES ·

The Legend of the Bluebonnet

CONTENTS:

Level 4
Theme 2: Encounters

The Comanche

The Comanche Indians lived in the southern Great Plains. They were hunters and traveled between Nebraska and northern Mexico following herds of buffalo. Buffalo provided them with meat for food and skins for clothing and shelter. The language and customs of the Comanche are similar to the Shoshoni, and scholars believe the two groups developed from the same ancestors.

The Comanche traveled and hunted on foot until the Spanish brought horses to North America in about 1700. The Comanche were great warriors and excelled at riding horses. Many learned to hang alongside or under their horses to avoid being hit by arrows or bullets!

Many Comanche died from disease in the early 1800s. In 1867, the Comanche agreed to live on a reservation in Oklahoma. Today, most of them still live in or near Lawton, Oklahoma. They own and share approximately 4,500 acres of land there with the Apache and Kiowa Indians.

The Comanche chief Quanah (1845?-1911) and a scene from Comanche life painted by George Catlin in 1834-35.

Our State Flowers

State	Flower
Alabama	Camellia
Alaska	Blue Forget-me-not
Arizona	Saguaro Cactus
Arkansas	Apple Blossom
California	Golden Poppy
Colorado	Rocky Mountain Columbine
Connecticut	Mountain Laurel
Delaware	Peach Blossom
Florida	Orange Blossom
Georgia	Cherokee Rose
Hawaii	Red Hibiscus
Idaho	Mock Orange
Illinois	Violet
Indiana	Peony
Iowa	Wild Rose
Kansas	Sunflower
Kentucky	Goldenrod
Louisiana	Magnolia
Maine	White Pine Cone
Maryland	Black-eyed Susan
Massachussetts	Mayflower
Michigan	Apple Blossom
Minnesota	Lady's Slipper
Mississippi	Magnolia
Missouri	Hawthorn